THAT GAME
FROM OUTER SPACE

The First Strange Thing That Happened to Oscar Noodleman

THAT GAME FROM OUTER SPACE

by Stephen Manes

illustrated by Tony Auth

E. P. DUTTON   NEW YORK

Library of Congress Cataloging in Publication Data

Manes, Stephen, date
That game from outer space.

Summary: Oscar becomes obsessed with the new video machine
in Hughie's pizza parlor and finds himself involved
in an unusual adventure with aliens from outer space.
[1. Video games—Fiction. 2. Extraterrestrial
beings—Fiction] I. Auth, Tony, ill. II. Title.
PZ7.M31264Th 1983 [Fic] 82-21144
ISBN 0-525-44056-9

Published in the United States by E. P. Dutton, Inc.,
2 Park Avenue, New York, N.Y. 10016

Published simultaneously in Canada by Clarke,
Irwin & Company Limited, Toronto and Vancouver

Editor: Ann Durell   Designer: Riki Levinson

Printed in the U.S.A.   First Edition
10 9 8 7 6 5 4 3 2 1

for Ron—
who keeps getting there first

1

It was the weirdest video game Oscar Noodle-man had ever seen. And the biggest. It was so tall it nearly touched the ceiling.

Oscar helped push it against the wall of the pizza parlor.

"What do you think?" asked Hughie.

Oscar didn't know what to think. It really looked more like a rocket ship than a video game. It was pointed at the top. It had fins at the bottom. It was painted bright yellow with green and purple stripes.

And Oscar noticed something else peculiar. "Where's the screen?" he asked.

"Watch this!" Hughie said. He put the plug into a socket. Suddenly the middle of the rocket ship opened up and spread way out to reveal a huge

control panel. The enormous screen seemed to wrap around Oscar's head. Hundreds of stars and asteroids and comets and planets and spaceships and strange buglike creatures were zooming and drifting every which way with noisy *blips* and *bloops* and *bleeps*. And in the very center of all that space traffic was a bright yellow rocket ship with green and purple stripes that somehow looked very familiar.

"Wow!" said Oscar, extremely impressed. "This really looks fantastic."

Hughie beamed with pride. "That's what I said the minute I found it. It's not every day something like this turns up at your back door." Hughie was the owner of Pete's Pizza Palace. He loved keeping up with the latest video games, even though he never played them himself.

Oscar noticed one slight problem with the machine. There was not a word of English on it anywhere. Everything from the control panel to the coin slot was labeled in some strange language that seemed to use squiggles instead of letters. He pointed this out to Hughie.

"I told you, I just found the game this morning," Hughie said. "When I came in, it was sitting in my parking space, right by the back door. I don't know where it came from. Maybe it's Japanese."

"I don't think so," Oscar said. He'd seen Japanese lettering in the instruction manual of the family car and on the bags of crackers his parents sometimes brought home, and these squiggles didn't look at all the same. "Maybe it's some sort of space language."

Hughie shook his head. "Don't bet your booties on it, buster. That's probably just a way to make it harder. Ought to bring in a lot of business."

Oscar went up to the machine and fiddled with the controls. "Maybe somebody ought to play the game a little. You know, just to check it out."

Hughie took the hint. "Somebody like you, for instance?"

Oscar shrugged. Hughie handed him a quarter. "You earned it helping me. Have fun."

Oscar thanked him and got ready to play. Oscar loved video games. He just didn't like having to pay for them. At one time he'd been spending every last cent of his allowance on the machines. But for months now he'd been saving most of his money to buy a game of his own, the kind he could hook up to his TV at home and play whenever he felt like it.

That's why he would hang around the Pizza Palace at odd hours when the place wasn't busy. Sometimes Hughie would have an errand for him to run, and Oscar would earn half a dollar for doing it. Sometimes Hughie would toss a quarter his way just to have company in the shop. And sometimes other kids would buy Oscar a game just so they could have somebody to beat. But those things didn't happen very often.

Which was why he felt so good now. Never before had Oscar been the very first person to try out a brand-new video game. He dropped his quarter in the slot and waited for something exciting to burst onto the screen.

Absolutely nothing happened.

"Hey, what's wrong?" he demanded.

"Maybe you have to press a button to get things going," Hughie suggested.

There were plenty of buttons on the control panel. Oscar tried the blue one and the green one and the red one. Not one of them did a thing. He tried pulling back on the control stick and pushing it forward. Nothing.

"Maybe it's a fifty-cent machine," Hughie said. He opened the cash register and tossed Oscar another quarter.

Oscar dropped it in the slot and tried all the controls again. Nothing happened—nothing at all.

"I hear there are some seventy-five-cent machines around," said Hughie. He threw Oscar another quarter.

Oscar dropped it in the slot and worked all the controls. The stars and comets and asteroids and bug creatures kept drifting and zooming across the screen, and the machine kept *blooping* and *bleeping* and *blurping* as if it couldn't have cared less.

"Now I know why somebody left this out back," Oscar said disgustedly. "It's broken."

Hughie leaned on his counter and looked the machine up and down. "You know what I think? I think this is the biggest video game I have ever seen. I think this must be a one-dollar machine."

He flipped Oscar still another quarter. Oscar was positive nothing would happen, but he stuck it in the slot.

With a rumble that was downright scary, the screen exploded into action. Dazzling colored blobs flashed on and off in every corner. Starships, asteroids, and space creatures whizzed in and out from all directions. The green-and-purple-striped yellow rocket ship blinked on and off. There was so much noise Oscar could hardly stand it.

"A dollar machine!" Hughie cried gleefully. "The first in the neighborhood! Maybe the first in the whole city!"

Oscar pushed the control stick. "It's working!" he shouted as the striped rocket ship on the screen zoomed forward through space. Then one of the big buglike creatures sped toward it. Oscar quickly yanked the stick to the left, and the ship made its escape.

A star cruiser swooped down from above. Oscar let it get close. Then he pushed on the stick and zipped away.

"See what that pedal's for," Hughie advised.

Oscar hadn't noticed it before. He ducked around a speeding asteroid, then put his foot on something that looked like the gas pedal of a car. When he pushed it down, the rocket ship went faster.

"Pretty classy," Hughie said proudly. "Nobody else has a game like this."

"Yeah," said Oscar, sneaking between two on-coming spaceships, "but what I can't figure out is what you're supposed to do now."

"Probably shoot down those aliens," Hughie said. "Try that blue button on the right."

Oscar pressed the blue button. A hazy blue cloud suddenly surrounded his rocket ship. Two creatures and an asteroid bumped into it and bounced away.

"Must be some sort of shield," Hughie declared.

"I wonder how come nobody ever shoots at me," Oscar said.

"Try the green button," Hughie suggested.

Oscar did. The rocket ship disappeared. A second or two later, it returned at the other end of the screen. As its blue cloud began to fade away, Oscar noticed a piece of drifting space junk in the neighborhood. Reaching for the green button, he made his ship disappear again. The space junk floated past harmlessly, and the rocket ship reappeared at the other end of the screen.

"You still haven't destroyed any aliens," Hughie pointed out.

Without the slightest warning, the picture on the screen abruptly changed. Everything but the

7

rocket ship had somehow grown bigger. Even the noise was louder. Oscar knew that could mean only one thing: He had reached the second level of the game!

Oscar could almost count the hairs on the huge legs of the buglike creatures. But he didn't have time for that. One of them seemed to be munching on a spaceship—and two more were headed his way!

Oscar steered his ship away from one huge mouth, but he nearly landed right in the jaws of the other. He hit the blue button just in time. The

cloud appeared, and the creature made a disappointed noise. It bounced off and drifted away without giving Oscar any trouble at all.

"Try the red button," Hughie recommended.

Oscar pressed his thumb into the red button. His rocket ship began firing brilliant beams of light. But as he turned the ship around to attack two nearby space creatures, they seemed to get angry.

Suddenly a star cruiser behind him fired two blinding laser blasts. In slightly less than an instant, Oscar's ship was destroyed.

The machine made a sad moan. The screen went blank. The game was over.

And then a yellow cockroach with green and purple stripes scooted down the outside of the screen and disappeared into the coin slot.

2

"Did you see that?" Oscar shouted.

"I guess you lost," said Hughie.

"I don't mean that. I mean that weird cockroach that ran down the outside of the screen."

"You mean those space creatures? The ones that look like bugs?"

"No! It looked something like them, but it wasn't just a picture. It was real. It was a yellow cockroach with green and purple stripes. Didn't you see it? It ran right into the coin slot."

Hughie got very indignant. "Listen, buster, I run a clean establishment. I don't have any cockroaches in this place, doggone it. Not even one. And certainly not any funny-colored ones. I don't think that's the least bit amusing."

Hughie walked over to the pizza board, kept

10

muttering "Doggone it!" and punched some dough. Obviously the subject of cockroaches was closed.

Oscar turned back to the game. The machine was *blipping* and *bleeping* and *blurping* just the way it had when it was first plugged in, and the screen had lit up again with asteroids and comets and buglike creatures drifting among the stars.

When he stopped to think about it, the game was really stupid. There didn't seem to be any rules, and if there were, you'd have to know how to read squiggles to understand them. The only other way to figure the game out would be to play it hundreds and hundreds of times. And that would cost—well, Oscar didn't even want to think about it. He had exactly one dollar and eighty-eight cents in his pocket, which was just enough for a slice of pizza and a small soda—his dinner, since his parents had to work late.

But Oscar didn't ask Hughie for a soda and a slice. Instead, he asked for four quarters for his dollar bill. Oscar couldn't begin to explain it, but in some strange way he felt he *had* to play the game, no matter how stupid it was, no matter what it cost. Somehow it had a grip on him. It wouldn't let him go.

But just as he was about to go back and play again, Mandy came through the door. Mandy was just about the only other kid his age still hanging around the neighborhood. Everybody else was away at summer camp.

11

"Far out! A new one!" she shrieked, rushing over to the yellow rocket ship with green and purple stripes.

"Yes, indeedy," Hughie said proudly.

"Anybody played it yet?"

"Just Oscar here."

"Good. It'll be easy to bop *his* name off the record."

Oscar hadn't thought of that. The other machines all let you punch your name in for everybody to see if you made the record score for that game. Oscar had never had his name up on any of the screens in his entire life.

But Mandy's name was on half the screens in the neighborhood. She was terrific at video games. Part of it was because her parents were divorced. Whenever her dad came to visit her, he always left her a bunch of rolls of quarters. She got to play more than anybody else around.

Oscar could tell she'd had one of those visits over the weekend. Her right pocket was bulging with what had to be her latest haul. It was so heavy it dragged her jeans down a little on that side.

"This looks like some game!" Mandy said. "How come your name's not up there, Oscar?"

Oscar really wished she'd go away. "I don't think it does that," he said.

"*Every* video game does that," Mandy insisted. "You probably did so bad on it that you didn't score any points. Zero's not a record in anything. That's why it didn't let you put your name up there."

Oscar shrugged. When he stopped to think about it, he really hadn't scored any points. At least, no numbers had gone up on the screen. He felt slightly embarrassed. He really wished he could play again before Mandy spoiled everything.

"What kind of lettering is this?" she demanded. "It looks like Russian or something."

"It's not Russian," Hughie declared. "My grandfather was Russian. If it were Russian, I'd know about it."

Mandy stared at the lettering, and then she stared at the screen. Mandy took video games very seriously. She believed in understanding everything she could about a game before she put her money in. She made Oscar explain all the controls.

Oscar reluctantly told her everything he knew. Then Mandy dropped a quarter in the slot and waited for something to happen.

"It costs a dollar," Oscar told her.

"A dollar! Forget it! I want my money back!"

"I don't think there's a coin return button," Oscar said. "If you don't want to play, I'll give you a quarter for the one you put in."

"Oh, I may as well see what's supposed to be so great about this machine," Mandy grumbled. She dug into her pocket, peeled three quarters from a fresh roll, and stuck them in the slot. The game rumbled and exploded just the way it had for Oscar.

Mandy pulled back on the stick, and the rocket ship roared through space. She turned the ship toward a nearby creature. She pressed the red button, and the rocket ship shot a bolt of light. But at the same instant, a star cruiser popped in

from above and blasted her ship with a laser beam. The machine moaned. The screen went dark. Game over.

"I don't see it asking you to put your name up there," Oscar said.

"Very funny," Mandy sniffed. "Watch this!" She took four quarters from her roll and put them in the slot. The game rumbled into action.

Mandy veered away from an oncoming cruiser. Then she used the blue cloud to hide from enemy invaders. But when she pressed the red button, her light-missile missed its target. One of the space creatures zoomed in and chewed up her cloud and her rocket ship. The machine seemed to chortle maliciously. Game over.

"Still no points," Oscar pointed out with delight.

"This game must be broken," Mandy wailed. "It's the stupidest one I've ever seen! And the most expensive. Play it all you want!"

And she took her quarters over to one of the old games, where her name was flashing on and off beside the highest score in the history of the machine.

3

Oscar fingered the change in his pocket. He felt the four quarters he'd gotten for his dollar bill, and he realized it would be really stupid to throw them down the slot of this particular video game. For one thing, it'd mean he'd have to go without dinner. Besides, what had happened to Mandy might very well happen to him and—bing!—his dollar would be gone just like that.

But then he began to get that funny feeling again. In a totally crazy way, Oscar felt sure the game was actually *asking* him to play it. He knew it couldn't be true—yet he was almost positive the electronic sounds had changed somehow ever since Mandy had left.

He stepped away a little just to see. The machine seemed to say "Come back! Come back!"—but without actually saying it.

Oscar couldn't help himself. He put his quarters in the slot and got ready for action. This time the screen lit up with the bigger ships and bigger aliens—the ones he'd been trying to handle when the game had gone dark on him.

One of those big buglike things was gaining on him from the right. Oscar moved his fingers toward the red button to get ready for a shot. But just as he was about to move his hand downward, the machine made a wild *bloop! bloop!* that seemed to be warning him not to. He hit the blue button instead, and the blue cloud enveloped his ship. Then he used the green button to disappear and turn up again at the other end of the screen.

The aliens and asteroids and comets kept coming at his ship from all directions. Some got so close that Oscar was positive they were going to crash into him. But Oscar kept using the stick and the foot pedal and the blue and green buttons, and somehow he always managed to dodge away.

Then—for no reason he could guess—the screen suddenly flashed with dazzling light, and Oscar seemed to be *inside* a rocket ship, zooming through space, looking through the windshield at cruisers and asteroids and creatures speeding *toward* him.

It was even more exciting than before. Oscar had to use a very delicate touch with the controls. He whizzed off to the side of some approaching asteroids. He dipped down below a speeding comet. He scooted around a few blobs of space junk.

And then a huge mouth began to fill the screen. It was ten times bigger than anything Oscar had met up with so far. He pulled back frantically on the stick to try to get past it, but no matter where he went, the giant jaws kept growing bigger. The mouth was monstrous, too big to go around in any direction. And Oscar had the feeling his pitiful light-weapons wouldn't be much good against it. Suddenly he remembered the green button. He pushed it hard.

The enormous jaws disappeared.

The screen went blank.

And then a skyful of stars appeared. Oscar saw that he was approaching a planet—a big green circle with white swirls on it. It looked a lot like the satellite photographs of Earth the weatherman showed on TV.

The planet was coming up fast. Oscar tried to steer around it, but the controls didn't seem to want to let him do that. He hoped he could keep from crashing. Leaning against the stick, he turned the ship around. Then he pressed his foot as hard as he could on the foot pedal to try to zoom away.

But the planet's gravity was too strong. The rocket ship began drifting backwards toward it. Oscar decided the green button was the only way out. He reached to his left for it.

The green button had disappeared!

There was no time to worry about it. As the ship drifted backwards, a little rearview screen appeared in the middle of the big screen. The planet filled the whole little screen, and as Oscar's ship got closer and closer, he could see he was coming down in an area of rocky hills. He steered the ship sideways, looking for a place to land. Then he saw a wide, flat area with lines painted on it. It looked suspiciously like a parking lot.

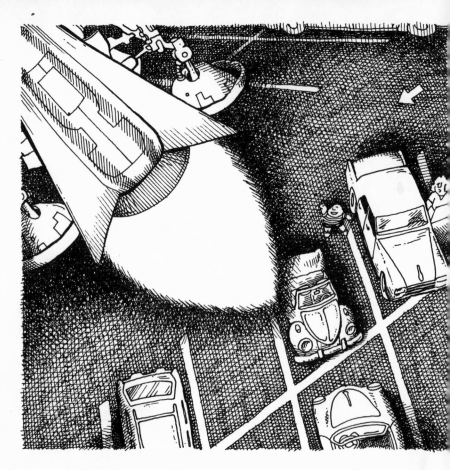

Oscar used the stick to keep the ship on course. But he was concentrating so hard on reaching the parking lot that his foot slipped off the pedal. He'd been pressing it to the floor to keep the ship from coming down too fast, and now the ship landed with a loud bang.

Oscar could almost feel the jolt. The screen went dark.

Oscar couldn't believe the game was over. He jiggled the control stick to try to get a picture. He

22

reached for the buttons. The blue one didn't do anything. The green one still wasn't there. But when he pressed the red one, the machine made a loud moan.

And then two yellow cockroaches with green and purple stripes scooted down the outside of the screen and disappeared into the coin slot. Oscar decided not to mention it to Hughie.

But what did it all mean? Were the cockroaches part of the game, or what? Oscar couldn't decide.

Suddenly the screen lit up again with its usual display of stars and comets and space creatures and gave off its usual *bleeps* and *bloops* and *blurps*. Except the sounds didn't seem quite the same as before. Oscar had no idea how he understood, but he was sure the machine was saying, "Play me again. It's serious! Important! Urgent! Put more money in!"

Wondering what to do, Oscar stood there until he couldn't stand it any longer. Heading for the door, he told Hughie he'd be right back. "No need to hurry," Mandy said from the game beside the door, and just to be mean, she stuck out her tongue at him and shot down five alien spaceships with one perfect laser blast.

4

The bank was right across the street. It was where Oscar kept the money he was saving up to buy his own video game. His account even paid interest.

The bank was closed except for the lobby. The lobby had a money machine that was open twenty-four hours a day. Oscar had a special card that let him use the machine to put money into his account —or take it out. He liked the machine because it was something like a video game—and it was free.

Oscar stuck his card into a slot. A little screen lit up with the words HI! HOW ARE YOU? WHAT CAN I DO FOR YOU?

Oscar pressed the button marked Balance. The screen lit up with the words HANG ON! I'LL SEE!

Actually, Oscar already knew how much money was in his account. He made it a point to stop by the bank and check on his money every couple of days just to see if the computer had made a mistake. He'd heard on TV about how one computer had accidentally added a million dollars to somebody's account, and he kept hoping it might happen to him. Oscar tried to imagine how he would feel if the screen lit up with the words YOU HAVE $1,000,087.36 IN YOUR SAVINGS AC-COUNT. But today, as usual, it simply read YOU HAVE $87.36.

WHAT ELSE CAN I DO FOR YOU? asked the screen.

Oscar just stood there. He stared at the button marked Withdraw Cash. It seemed to be pulling him toward it and yet pushing him away at the same time. On the one hand, he knew he really shouldn't touch any of the money it had taken him so long to save. On the other hand, that game across the street was acting as though there'd be some terrible emergency if he didn't play it.

WHAT ELSE CAN I DO FOR YOU? began blinking on and off. The machine was getting impatient.

Oscar made a face and pressed the Withdraw Cash button.

HOW MUCH? the screen asked. $20? $30? $50? $100? There was a button beside each figure.

Oscar knew the $100 button was out of the question. He'd tried it before. If he pressed it, the screen would tell him WHOOPS! SORRY! YOU DON'T HAVE ENOUGH MONEY IN YOUR ACCOUNT!

The other three buttons were still possible, though. Oscar knew the sensible thing would be to press the Start Over button and walk away, leaving all his money in the account. The second most sensible thing would be to press the button marked $20. If he needed more money later, he could always come back and get it. The computer banking center was always open.

Oscar had a sinking feeling as he pressed the button marked $50. The screen lit up with the message he expected: PLEASE TELL ME YOUR PERSONAL CODE.

He hesitated. He still wasn't sure he wanted to go through with this. But finally he punched his personal code on a little keyboard beside the machine. His personal code was SPACEMAN.

The screen said THANK YOU. The machine made a clanking noise, and a big metal drum revolved with a whir. Then the drum opened to reveal two crisp twenty-dollar bills and one slightly rumpled ten. PLEASE TAKE YOUR MONEY, the screen commanded.

Oscar did. The drum clanked again and then whirred shut.

MAY I DO ANYTHING ELSE TO SERVE

YOU? the screen inquired politely. Oscar put the money in his wallet and pressed the **No** button.

WOULD YOU LIKE A RECEIPT?

Oscar pressed **Yes**. The machine made a noise as though it were chewing some sort of crunchy cereal, and then it spit out a little ticket. The ticket had the date and time on it, and, below that, **RE-CEIVED FROM SAVINGS $50.00. THANK YOU. HAVE A NICE DAY.**

Oscar had the feeling he wasn't going to have a nice day at all. He had the feeling that what he

should do was fill out a deposit slip this very instant and put the money back into his savings account.

But he went back across the street to Pete's Pizza
Palace.

5

"It's not Japanese," said Hughie, who was cleaning the pizza oven as Oscar came through the door. "A Japanese lady just came in for a slice, and she told me so herself. It's also not Chinese or Arabic or any other language she's ever heard of, and she's heard quite a few. She teaches languages at the University. What do you think of that?"

"Interesting," Oscar said. But he felt worried. For some reason, he didn't think anybody should be playing the game but him. "Did she play the game?" he asked.

"Do busy professors usually play video games?" Hughie asked. "Does this video game come from Japan? Are there cockroaches in my pizza shop? Same answers: no, no, and uh-uh!"

Oscar didn't say anything about the cockroaches.

He just asked Hughie to change his ten-dollar bill into quarters.

Hughie put down his sponge and opened the cash register. "Your friend Mandy told me I ought to get rid of that new game. Maybe she's right. After all, she *is* an expert.

"Mandy doesn't know everything," Oscar said as Hughie handed him a roll of quarters. "I like that game."

Hughie grinned. "She's probably mad at it because it wouldn't let her put her name up there."

"You got it," Oscar said, heading back to the big yellow rocket ship with the green and purple stripes. It might have been his imagination, but he really thought he could hear it begin to get excited as he got closer. It was as though the *bloops* and *bleeps* and *blurps* were saying "Hooray! Oscar's back!"

The roll of quarters felt heavy in Oscar's hand. Slowly he peeled back the paper from one end and used his thumbnail to pry four quarters loose. Then he put the roll into his pocket and dropped the four quarters in the slot one by one.

What replaced the stars and asteroids and comets on the screen was a strange picture that Oscar didn't recognize at first. It looked kind of the way skyscrapers do when you stare up at them from the street. But these skyscrapers were moving.

Suddenly Oscar realized the skyscrapers had two legs each. And two arms. And—very tiny, way up

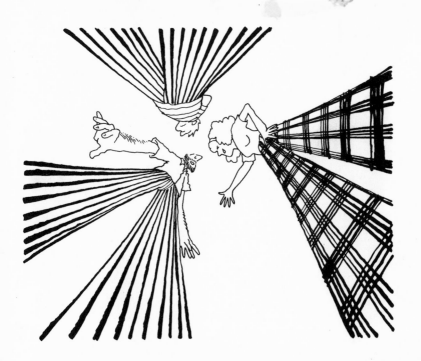

in the sky—faces. The skyscrapers were *people*—
from a bug's eye view.

As Oscar stared in amazement, he spotted an
enormous foot walking toward him. Pushing hard
on the control stick and pressing the foot pedal to
the floor, he crawled forward—just in time to avoid
being crushed by a size 1800 heel! He scooted into
a corner to get away. Then he began creeping up
a wall.

It was the craziest game Oscar had ever played in
his entire life. Way across the room on the screen,
he could see a huge monster's enormous feet strid-
ing toward him.

Oscar scurried up to the ceiling. Now he had an upside-down view of the world—which included a human who was using what seemed to be the end of a redwood tree to try and squash him.

Oscar zigzagged left and right, keeping one step ahead of the menacing tree—which he realized was actually a broomstick. Then the human disappeared, and Oscar crept to the other side of the ceiling.

But as he reached the far wall, the air suddenly became filled with big, shimmering drops of liquid. Through these horrible balloon-size raindrops, he could see the human below. The drops were coming from a spray can aimed in Oscar's direction.

His only hope was to slip into a crack halfway down the wall.

Oscar hurried toward it, dodging the enormous globules flying his way. As he got near the crack, he zigged out of the way of the biggest, shiniest droplet yet. But he zagged straight into another one.

The machine *blooped* sadly, and the screen went dark. The game was over.

Oscar reached into his pocket for his roll of quarters without even stopping to think about it. Half a dozen yellow cockroaches with green and purple stripes ran across the outside of the screen and disappeared down the coin slot.

6

Oscar realized he'd *better* stop to think. Something extremely peculiar was going on. It didn't even begin to make sense. Yet in some crazy way it all made perfect sense.

What did the cockroaches running across the screen have to do with the bug-beings in the game? Why were they the same color as the machine? Why did they keep slipping through the coin slot? Were they real, or were they illusions—or were they mechanical cockroaches that were somehow part of the game?

Oscar tried to sort it out in his head. Maybe the roaches were a way of showing your score. The more roaches, the better you'd done. Obviously he was improving: First one cockroach had gone by, then two, and now six. And each time they seemed to be getting bigger. Mandy hadn't gotten even one, not even a baby one.

Oscar decided he was on the right track. Even the machine seemed to be telling him so. Or was he just imagining that the *bleeps* and *blips* and *blurps* and *bloops* were telling him to put his quarters in and play? Was it just some clever, tricky way of getting him to waste his money?

Oscar stopped thinking and dropped four quarters in the coin slot.

The screen lit up with a bug's-eye view again. This time Oscar the Bug was inside what looked like a long dark tunnel. There was absolutely no way he could have recognized it—he'd certainly never been anywhere like it before—but somehow he knew exactly where he must be. He was inside the walls of a house or some sort of building—and it was almost pitch-black. Oscar decided to creep along slowly, crawling carefully over the beams and huge water pipes that got in his way. He made very sure not to get too close to the electrical wires. And when he saw a narrow opening beneath his feet, he slowly and carefully squeezed into it.

"Hey, Oscar!" Hughie called. "It's nearly closing time!"

"What?" Oscar cried as he wiggled through the crack.

"It's Monday, remember?"

Oscar found himself in a big kitchen cupboard. As he kept crawling forward, he let out a deep sigh.

He knew all about Monday. Monday was the day Hughie closed the place early. There was really no good reason for it, but it was a tradition left over from the original Pete, who'd opened the place years ago. The faded sign on the door said OPEN DAILY 11–11 EXCEPT MON. 11–7:00, and Hughie didn't want to change it. He claimed that might bring him bad luck, so he always closed up at 7:00 on Mondays.

"But I haven't finished this game yet," Oscar moaned, creeping along the kitchen shelf past a big bag of potato chips.

"Well, hurry up," Hughie told him. "I want to get home to Pupkins." Pupkins was Hughie's enormous German shepherd. He was famous in the neighborhood for his unpleasant temper and bad breath.

"Can't Pupkins wait?" Oscar said, slinking carefully around a tall bottle of ketchup. "This cost me a dollar. I can't just give up now."

Hughie let out a deep sigh. "How long do you think it'll take?"

"How should I know?" Oscar said. "You know the way these games work. You get to play as long as you're doing good. And I'm doing great."

"Well, I can't stay here forever. Pupkins will get cranky."

The machine made a noise as if to say Oscar had just made some sort of miraculous score. Oscar couldn't see what he'd done that was so wonderful,

except climb up the side of a box of saltines, but he didn't complain. "I think this means extra playing time," he said.

"Look," Hughie told him, "tell you what. I've got to go over to the bank and deposit the money from the register. I'll leave the place open till I come back."

"Don't rush," Oscar said.

"Very funny," Hughie sniffed. "Just remember, if anybody comes in, tell 'em we're closed."

"Okay," said Oscar, reaching the top of the box of saltines.

"Remember, just this one game, and that's it, buster."

"Right," Oscar said as Hughie went out the door.

At that moment a strange thought popped into Oscar's head. He wondered if he could just sort of *fly* down from the top of the saltine box to the shelf far below. "After all, bugs have wings," he said to himself.

He decided to try it. He made his way to the edge of the saltine box. Then he pushed forward on the stick and leaped off.

He floated down gently, sort of as if he had a parachute. He could almost feel his soft landing, even though it was only a game.

Without warning, the machine suddenly blasted out a fanfare so loud it hurt Oscar's ears. The screen went dark. The two biggest green-and-purple-striped yellow cockroaches Oscar had ever seen marched with great dignity straight down the outside of the screen. Then they stopped right in the middle, wiggled their antennae, and stared at him.

7

Oscar froze. He had never been much of a fan of cockroaches, and now two the size of candy bars were standing right beneath his nose and staring at him. The fanfare stopped. There was total silence. Oscar did not like the look of this at all.

The cockroach on the left was the bigger of the two. It wiggled an antenna. "Nice go," said a gurgly electronic-sounding voice that spoke English in an accent Oscar vaguely recognized. "You win."

Oscar was too stupefied to reply.

The smaller cockroach—it wasn't *much* smaller—twitched its right front leg. "How about giving us a hand?" asked a similar but deeper voice.

Oscar could barely get three words out. "Who? Are? You?"

The bigger cockroach scratched its head. "Haven't you figured that out by now?"

Oscar shook his head.

"What if we told you we're creatures from outer space? What would you say to that, buster?"

"You look more like cockroaches to me," was what Oscar said to that.

The bigger cockroach stamped four of its six feet indignantly. "Are cockroaches yellow with green and purple stripes?"

"Well . . ." Oscar stammered.

"Do cockroaches spend their time standing around talking to people?"

"I guess not," Oscar admitted.

"Sure, we're aware that some animals on this planet of yours do resemble us slightly. But they happen to be pretty stupid. We're not. How many cockroaches do you know who can pick up your language by hanging around a pizza store? Huh, buster?"

That was the accent Oscar recognized—*Hughie's* accent! "What do you want?" Oscar asked.

"We want you to help us."

"Help you? How?" Oscar suddenly had the feeling that these intelligent talking bugs might be planning to take over the entire world.

"We want to get out of here."

"Can't you just—I don't know—crawl?"

The bug on the right made a hissing noise as if to say that Oscar's remark was the stupidest thing it had ever heard. "What we mean is, we want to leave this planet."

"Oh," said Oscar.

40

"Our space vehicle is on the blink. We need some help to fix it."

"Me?" Oscar squeaked.

"Why not?"

"But I don't know anything about space vehicles. I have trouble doing stuff with my bicycle."

"Have no fear. We'll tell you exactly what to do."

"Why me? Why not somebody who knows all about spaceships?"

"Because you are exactly the person we've been looking for," said the smaller bug with a chuckle.

"Huh?" Oscar said.

The smaller bug took one step forward. "As captain of this ship, it's my duty to get my crew home safely. But, doggone it"—they'd certainly learned their English from Hughie, all right—"we've run into some engine trouble. On most planets, we'd just bop into a garage and have it taken care of. But

here, since we look something like those animals you call cockroaches, it's not that simple. Whenever humans see us, they get terribly upset. Two of my crew were nearly crushed to death."

"Cockroaches aren't exactly people's favorite animals," Oscar explained.

"I'll say!" the captain went on. "We can't figure it out. They don't bite people. They don't kill other animals. They clean up what others leave behind. They just don't have a whole lot of smarts—but then, neither do a lot of people."

"Cockroaches carry diseases," Oscar declared.

"And people don't? Did you ever hear of something called a 'cold'? This is the only planet where we've run into it. And there doesn't seem to be any cure. For two weeks, our crew was coughing and sneezing."

"You still haven't answered my question," Oscar said, changing the subject. "Why me?"

The captain's companion stepped forward. "Okay, buster. We've been traveling all over your world in this machine. Ever since the engine went kaflooey, we've only had enough power to go from place to place—but not enough to escape your planet's gravity. We need help. But we can't trust just anybody."

"So we set up this test—this 'game,' as you call it—to weed out the people we can't trust," the captain continued. "All over your world, people seem to think the way to solve problems is to use force

—deadly force, like that red button over there. But the minute you touch that button on *this* game, you lose."

"I sort of figured that out," Oscar said modestly.

"And you should be proud," said the captain. "You're only the third person in the entire world who did."

Oscar blushed a little. "Then why didn't you let the first two people help you?"

"Because they failed the second part of the test. As soon as the game changed from spaceships and asteroids to living like one of us, they got bored. They quit playing."

"But you didn't," the smaller bug put in. "That proved you have curiosity. It also showed us that you might be able to understand us."

Oscar felt flattered. "But what do you want me to do, exactly? I told you, I don't know anything at all about fixing spaceships."

"You don't have to. We'll tell you what to do."

"How come you can't do it yourself?"

The bigger bug shifted uneasily from side to side. "Well . . . it's kind of embarrassing to say this, but . . . we're too little."

The captain nodded. "The way this ship is built, we need special power tools for some kinds of repairs. And somebody back home forgot to pack the tools. You can bet we'll have plenty to say to her when we return."

"But I don't have any special power tools,"

Oscar protested. "I don't even have any ordinary ones."

The bugs giggled and laughed as if they'd never heard anything so funny in the entire universe. "Of course you do. Just look at the ends of your arms."

Oscar looked. "My . . . hands?"

"Precisely."

The bugs began making a low chirping sound, as if they were talking to each other in secret, as if they didn't want Oscar to hear. Then the voices piped up again. "Listen, that guy who makes the pizza is coming back."

Oscar glanced out the door. Hughie was way across the street. Apparently the bugs had super-sharp hearing. "Figure out a way to get rid of him for a while so you can fix our engines," the captain urged. "He's definitely one person who wouldn't understand."

"I don't know . . ." Oscar said.

"You'll be helping a good cause," the bugs chirped in unison.

"But it's his store. I *can't* just get rid of him."

"You'll think of something."

"But I'm just a kid," Oscar said. "Maybe you should get some scientists to help you. They'd probably like to study you, too."

"Study us? More likely they'd *step* on us," said the captain. "Phooey on your scientists!"

Oscar looked across the street. Hughie was still

taking his time, waddling along. Oscar had one last question for the bugs. "You sure you're not going to try to take over the world?"

The bugs laughed helplessly. Finally the captain said, "Friend, of all the worlds we've been to, this is the last one we'd ever think of taking over. All we want to do is get out of here."

"I still don't know . . ." Oscar responded.

"We'll do something nice for you," the captain said.

"Yeah, but . . ."

"We'll *pay* you!" cried the other bug in desperation. And as Hughie came through the door, the captain and his—or was it *her?*—companion scrambled down the screen toward the coin slot. Oscar was positive the slot was too small for them to squeeze through.

But it wasn't.

8

The screen lit up again with its usual outer space scene, but the *bleeps* and *blips* and *bloops* somehow told Oscar that he'd better not stop to dig into his pocket for money. The bugs would let him play for free this time.

Oscar pushed forward on the control stick to get the rocket ship away from a giant space cruiser. He tried to look as if he were concentrating hard on the game, but actually he was concentrating hard on just what he would say to Hughie.

"Anybody come in?" Hughie asked.

"Nope," Oscar said, moving out of the way of an asteroid.

Hughie came over and stood behind him. "How's it going?"

"I'm really doing great," Oscar said. "There's no telling how much time I've got left."

"Yes, there is," Hughie said. "You've got exactly thirty seconds left, buster, because that's how long till I close up shop."

"Aw, come on," Oscar pleaded, scooting deftly around a space creature. "Not just when I'm going good."

"Everybody always says that," said Hughie.

"Not me. This is the first time this has ever happened. And besides, this is a dollar machine. I've got a lot invested here." Sneaking around a comet, Oscar prayed that Hughie would reconsider.

"Look, fair is fair," Hughie said. "Wrap it up and I'll give you a dollar. You can start over fresh tomorrow."

"Yeah, but probably I won't do this good tomorrow. Come on, Hughie. Please?"

Keeping one eye on the screen, Oscar shot a glance at Hughie. Hughie was scratching his chin, thinking it over. Oscar leaned on the control stick, pushed the foot pedal down, and zipped around an asteroid.

"Tell you what," Hughie said. "You can stick around for a while. I'll just lock the bottom lock. That one'll let you out—but once you're out, it won't let you back in."

"Thanks, Hughie," Oscar said, breathing a sigh of relief. The machine seemed to sigh itself.

"Wait a second, I'm not through," Hughie went on. "I'll come back and lock up for good when I take Pupkins for his walk in half an hour or so. If you're not done by then, tough tomato sauce. So make it snappy."

Oscar and the machine gave slightly worried gasps, but Hughie didn't seem to notice. "Remember," he said as he went out the door, "half an hour. If you leave before then, make sure you pull the door shut tight."

"Right," Oscar said as Hughie went through the door. As the screen went dark, Oscar looked at the clock and made a mental note of the time. The clock said 7:06.

The two big bugs scooted to the middle of the screen. "Good work," they said. "What does 'tough tomato sauce' mean?"

"Forget about 'tough tomato sauce,' " Oscar said. "He won't be gone long."

48

"It shouldn't take long to fix us up," the captain said.

"By the way, didn't you say something about paying me?" Oscar inquired.

"Humans!" huffed the captain. "Where we come from, everybody trusts everybody else."

"Not here," Oscar pointed out.

"First things first," said the bigger bug. "Fix our engine, and then we'll pay you. Honest."

Oscar hoped he could trust them. He decided to take a chance. "Okay," he said. "What do you want me to do?"

"Go around to the back of the machine," the captain said and led the way. Oscar followed.

"You see that red knob?" the captain asked.

Oscar pointed. "That one?" It looked like the handle of a water faucet.

"Right."

"Yeah."

"Okay. We're going to start our engines. When you hear them rev up, start turning the knob to the right."

The rocket ship made a couple of *bloops* and *bleeps*, and then a rumbling noise began. "Now!" the captain cried. Oscar turned the knob slowly to the right.

The rumbling grew louder. "Farther!" the captain shouted.

The knob began to get stiff, hard to turn. Oscar put all his strength behind it. "See what we mean about those power tools?" the captain shouted over the noise.

Oscar nodded and kept turning.

"More!" cried the captain. With all his might, Oscar forced the knob forward one last tiny bit. It was the best he could do.

"Okay!" the captain shouted. "Stop!"

The engines were positively roaring now. The captain gestured with one antenna for Oscar to follow him back up front.

Oscar did. When he got there, he was welcomed by hundreds and hundreds of yellow bugs with green and purple stripes marching in formation up and down the screen. Suddenly they stopped and twitched their antennae in unison. Above the roar of the engines, Oscar could hear them shouting and cheering. "Thanks, buster!" they hollered in unison. "You did it!"

Oscar nodded politely.

Then the captain stepped forward. "Really, we're very grateful. If you ever take a vacation in space, please come visit us. I'm sure you'd enjoy our planet, even if you found the beds a trifle small."

Suddenly the coin slot opened outward, and dozens of coins came spilling out. Oscar was overjoyed to find those quarters of his that he thought he'd never see again—not to mention the money Mandy had put in. But the rest of the coins were from other places: France, Nigeria, Denmark, and countries whose names were in writing he couldn't read. The bugs had been telling the truth: They really had traveled all over the world.

"We thank you from the bottom of our hearts," said the captain. "Now you are rich beyond your wildest dreams."

Oscar guessed that all the coins put together

probably wouldn't amount to more than twenty dollars or so, but to the bugs they were so large they probably seemed like millions. Oscar didn't want to hurt his new friends' feelings. "Thank you," he said as sincerely as he could. He put the quarters in his pocket and went behind the counter to get a paper bag for the rest of the coins.

"Don't mention it," said the captain's big companion. "We couldn't take off with all that extra weight anyhow. Now is there anything else we can help with before we leave?"

Oscar tried to think of something. He thought hard. Then a terrific idea popped into his head. "Do you know how to work those video games over there?"

"We're not strong enough to push the buttons," said the captain.

"I mean from the inside."

"I suppose so. Compared to a spaceship, they must be simple."

"Well . . ." Oscar said hesitantly.

"Don't take forever, friend. We do have to be going."

"Do you think you could put my name up there on the screens—you know, for the highest score?"

The captain wiggled its antennae. "Not terribly honest, is it?"

"Well . . ."

"Humans!" snorted the captain's companion.

"Never mind," said the captain. And the next thing Oscar knew, he saw four smallish bugs glide down to the ground, scoot over to the machines, climb up the sides, and jump into the coin slots. "How do you spell it?" the captain asked.

As Oscar called out "O-S-C-A-R-J-N-O-O-D-L-E-M-A-N," he saw his name appear on all four video screens at once. Mandy's name disappeared. And the bugs had given him scores that were impossible to beat—scores that were ten times Mandy's best. The four bugs jumped to the floor from the coin slots and scurried back to their ship.

"Thanks," Oscar said, grinning. "Thanks a lot."

"No problem," said the captain. "It really is kind of sneaky of you, though."

"Could I ask one more question?" Oscar asked.

"Make it snappy."

"What language is that?" Oscar asked.

" 'Make it snappy'? We thought it was English."

"No, not *that* language. The language on these labels. These squiggles."

The whole screenful of roaches sent up a giggle. "People all over your world wonder about that!" exclaimed the captain. "It's no language. It's just squiggles. We figured people would be so curious about it, they'd try the game. We were right, too."

"Oh," Oscar said.

"Anything else?" the big insect asked.

Oscar shook his head.

"Well, then," said the captain.

All the roaches sent up a final cheer. Then they lined up two by two, marched down the screen, and hopped into the coin slot.

The captain was the last to disappear. Then he—
or was it she?—stuck his—or was it her?—head
back out.

"When you see the signal," the captain said,
"press the green button."

"What's the signal?" Oscar asked.

"You'll know it when you see it."

The captain's antennae disappeared down the
coin slot. Oscar felt a shivery twinge of sadness.
And a touch of worry—the clock read 7:35.

Suddenly the roar of the engines grew even
louder. A huge picture of a finger pressing a green
button appeared on the screen. That, obviously,
was the signal.

Oscar pressed the green button. The screen gently folded up and snapped shut. The roar stopped.
For a long moment everything was still. Then
with a screaming whine that made Oscar cover
his ears with his hands, the yellow rocket ship
with green and purple stripes simply vanished.

9

Oscar just stood there. He wasn't sure if he was awake or dreaming. He kept staring at the spot where the rocket ship had been.

Then he heard a key turning in the lock. It was Hughie.

"How'd you do with your game?" Hughie asked as Pupkins dragged him through the door.

Pupkins put his feet on Oscar's shoulders and licked Oscar's face. "Oh . . . uh . . ." Oscar stammered, backing away from Pupkins' terrible breath.

"Hey, what happened? Where'd it go?" Hughie shrieked.

Oscar knew he'd have to think fast. "Well . . . uh . . ."

"Well, what? It didn't just walk away!"

"No," Oscar agreed.

"And it certainly didn't take off like a spaceship."

"Not exactly," Oscar said.

"So where *did* it go?"

Hughie and Pupkins were staring at Oscar so fiercely he thought they both might bite him. "They came to take it back," Oscar blurted out, wondering what in the world he'd say next.

"Who? Who came to take it back?"

"The company. People from the company. People from the company that made it."

"Why?" cried Hughie, looking as though he might tear his hair out. "Why?"

"They said they had to recall it. They said it wasn't working right. They said it wasn't safe. They left it out back by mistake."

"Oh," said Hughie, deflating like a punctured balloon.

"When I won, it gave me all the money inside," Oscar said, holding up his bag of coins and shaking it. "They said it wasn't supposed to do that."

"I'll say," said Hughie, leaning against the counter for support. "I wonder what else was wrong with it."

Oscar shrugged. "I don't know. I guess it had a few bugs in it."

The sun was beginning to go down. As Hughie locked up the shop, Oscar went across the street to the bank. Inside, he checked his account on the machine. He was hoping that maybe the space bugs had done him one last surprise favor and fixed the machine so that his account would show an extra million dollars or so, the way they'd put his name up on the video games. But the screen showed exactly $37.36 in Oscar's account—precisely what it was supposed to. Oscar decided that putting an extra million dollars into his account was probably not honest enough for the insects from outer space.

Oscar filled out a deposit slip and put his two twenty-dollar bills back into his account. When the bank opened tomorrow, he could put back the other ten—the machine wouldn't accept coins. But now he'd have to think of something different to do with his savings. He certainly wasn't going to use the money to buy some ordinary video game. After what had happened to him, regular video games seemed kind of—well, *tame.*

Oscar went back across the street and peered through the windows of the pizza shop. The only light inside was the glow of the video games—with **HIGH SCORE: OSCAR J NOODLEMAN** on every screen.

Was it real or was it a dream? Even though he was holding his bagful of unusual foreign coins, Oscar still wasn't positive. While he was thinking it over, he saw a cockroach the size of a golf ball crawl halfway down one of the video screens and stop right in the middle.

Oscar looked closer. The cockroach was not yellow with green and purple stripes. It was brown. But it did seem to be wiggling its antennae at Oscar.

Oscar waved back. The bug didn't seem to notice. It floated down to the floor, crawled across the room, and climbed up to the counter.

Oscar decided not to mention it to Hughie.